CAPTAIN AWESOME, THE SHOW MUST GO ON!

By STAN KIRBY

Illustrated by DOC MORAN

LITTLE SIMON

New York   London   Toronto   Sydney   New Delhi

LITTLE SIMON

An imprint of Simon & Schuster Children's Publishing Division • 1230 Avenue of the Americas, New York, New York 10020 • First Little Simon paperback edition September 2021 • Copyright © 2021 by Simon & Schuster, Inc. • Also available in a Little Simon hardcover edition. • All rights reserved, including the right of reproduction in whole or in part in any form. • LITTLE SIMON is a registered trademark of Simon & Schuster, Inc., and associated colophon is a trademark of Simon & Schuster, Inc. • For information about special discounts for bulk purchases, please contact Simon & Schuster Special Sales at 1-866-506-1949 or business@simonandschuster.com. • The Simon & Schuster Speakers Bureau can bring authors to your live event. • For more information or to book an event, contact the Simon & Schuster Speakers Bureau at 1-866-248-3049 or visit our website at www.simonspeakers.com. • Designed by Gabrielle Chang. • The text of this book was set in Little Simon Gazette.

Manufactured in the United States of America 0821 MTN

10 9 8 7 6 5 4 3 2 1

Library of Congress Cataloging-in-Publication Data

Names: Kirby, Stan, author. | Moran, Doc, illustrator.

Title: The show must go on! / by Stan Kirby; illustrated by Doc Moran.

Description: First Little Simon paperback edition. | New York: Little Simon, 2021. | Series: Captain Awesome; 23 | Audience: Ages 5–9. | Summary: During a school field trip to Sunnyview Playhouse, Captain Awesome and his friends spring into action after seeing a mysterious Man in Black who seems to be stealing jewels.

Identifiers: LCCN 2020051538 (print) | LCCN 2020051539 (ebook) | ISBN 9781534493315 (hardcover) | ISBN 9781534493308 (paperback) | ISBN 9781534493322 (ebook) | Subjects: CYAC: Superheroes—Fiction. | Stealing—Fiction. | Theater—Fiction. | School field trips—Fiction. | Classification: LCC PZ7.K633529 Sho 2021 (print) | LCC PZ7.K633529 (ebook) | DDC [Fic]—dc23

LC record available at https://lccn.loc.gov/2020051538

Table of Contents

CHAPTER 1

The Playhouse of Bore-doom

ZZZZ

By
Eugene

If Billy has three apples and eats ten more while on an eight-hour flight from New York to Paris, how many apples would he eat on a fourteen-hour flight to Tokyo?"

BLAH, BLAH, BLAH.

Eugene McGillicudy hated word problems. It always felt like the words came at him faster than a laser attack from Lord Laser Blast!

"Um, who's Billy again?" Eugene's best friend, Charlie Thomas Jones, asked.

Sally Williams, who was sitting behind Charlie, shrugged. "Beats me, but the bigger question is . . . why are Billy's apples going to France?"

"Hold on a second," Eugene chimed in. There was a more pressing problem than worrying about Billy's apples. "What's wrong with that clock?"

The second hand on the clock was twitching as if it had an ant down its pants.

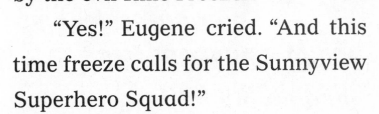

"Oh, this can only mean one thing!" Charlie exclaimed. "Time has been frozen by the evil Time Freezer!"

"Yes!" Eugene cried. "And this time freeze calls for the Sunnyview Superhero Squad!"

Wait. Time-out.

You've never heard of the Sunnyview Superhero Squad? Well, here's a quick rundown: Inspired by Super Dude, their favorite comic book hero, Eugene, Charlie, and Sally all have secret superhero identities: *CAPTAIN AWESOME*, *NACHO CHEESE MAN*, and *SUPERSONIC SAL!* Together, they keep Sunnyview safe from evil.

"Quick, we need to start that clock!" Eugene yelled. So the trio closed their eyes to

THINK!
THINK!
THINK!

Absolutely nothing happened until . . .

DING!

The lunch bell went off!

"Hurry! We need to get away while we can!" Eugene said as he got up. But then he stopped in his tracks.

"Wait a minute," Ms. Beasley said. "Before you go to lunch, I have a special announcement. We're going on a field trip on Friday!"

YES! FINALLY!

Maybe they were going to the Sunnyview Amusement Park!

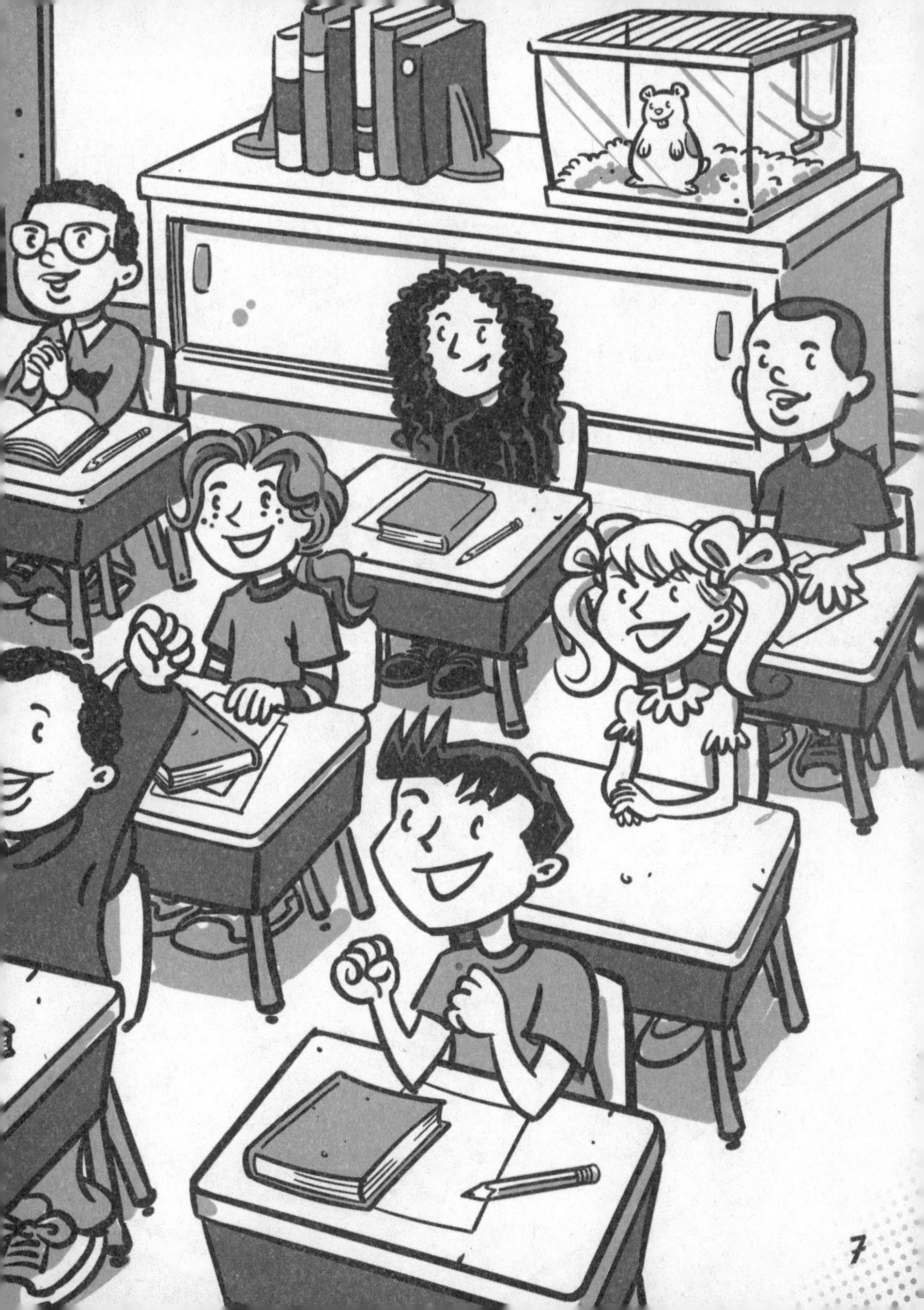

"Get ready, class. We'll be going to the Sunnyview . . . Playhouse!"

Rats! So close but SO far, Eugene thought.

"Aren't plays for old people?" Charlie asked.

"Like our parents?" Eugene added.

"Oh no, boys," Ms. Beasley replied. "Watching a play is a fun activity for all ages!"

Then Ms. Beasley opened her arms and sang out, *"FAHHH-LA-LAAAAAAALALA!"*

Right away, his teacher's voice reminded Eugene of Super Dude No. 29, which was about Sing-along Kong, the singing gorilla.

Eugene slumped down into his seat because he knew that this time, not even Super Dude could save them from going on this field trip of bore-doom.

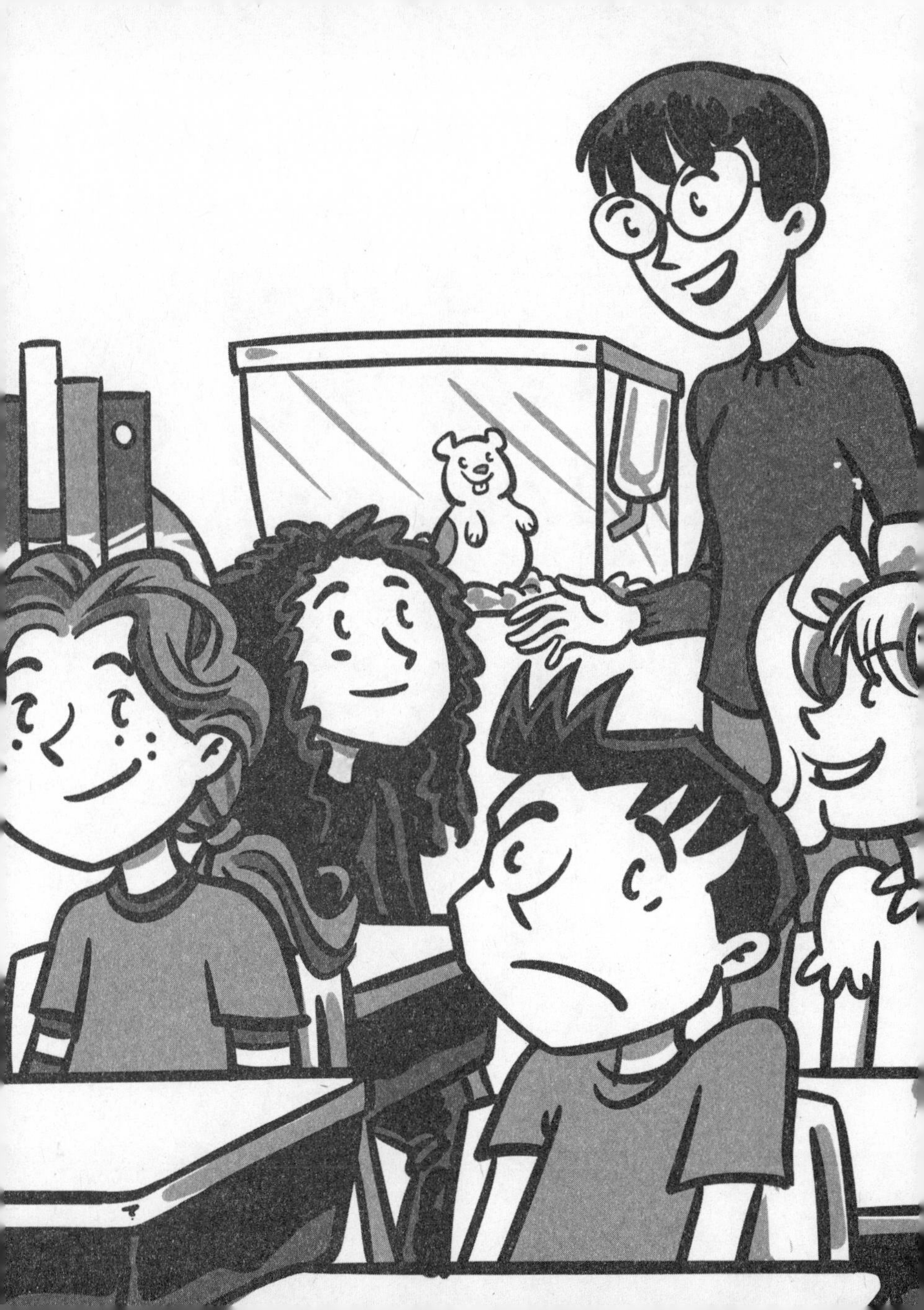

CHAPTER 2

Friday Is the Perfect Day for a Playdate!

By Eugene

A thick layer of dread hung over Eugene and Charlie as they got on the bus for the field trip.

Unlike her two friends, Sally was in a great mood.

"Are you guys ready for this bus ride?" she asked excitedly.

"Well, that depends on where this bus takes us." Eugene sighed as he looked over at Charlie. "Did you bring your cheese?"

Charlie patted his backpack. "Yeah, I've got plenty of nacho cheese and some Extra Kooler Ranch, too."

"Perfect! I brought my Boredom Destruction Kit!" Eugene opened his backpack and placed it on the seat. "I've got Super Dude comic books, markers, coloring books, puzzles, and lots of candy and snacks to help us stay awake."

Just as Eugene was opening a bag of chips, Meredith Mooney popped up over the seat. "Oh, Ms. Beasley!" she cried out. "Eugene and Charlie are eating FOOD on the bus!"

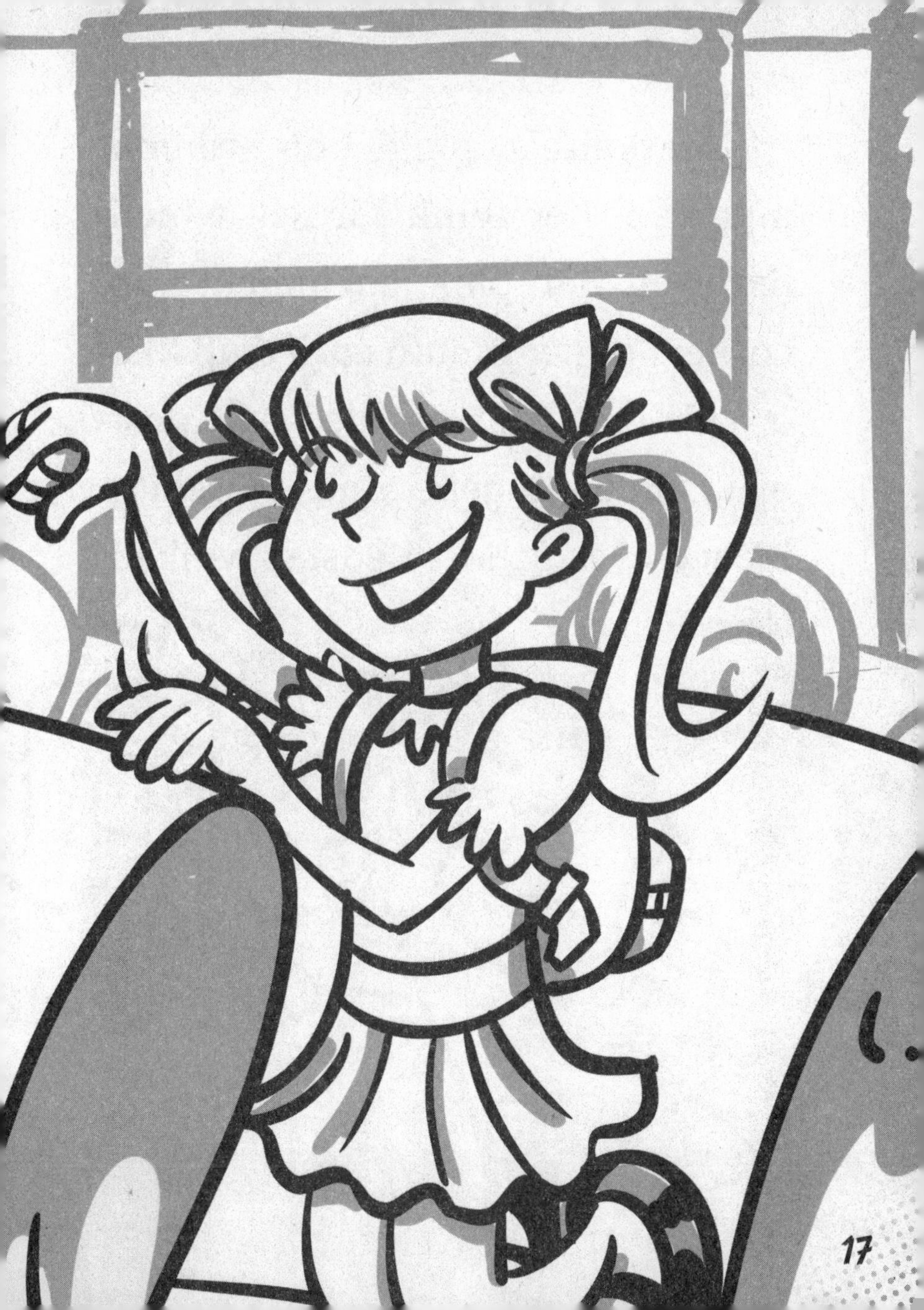

Meredith's pink hair ribbon matched her pink dress, which matched her pink backpack. The corners of her mouth curled up like a cat's tail as she smiled her most evil smile. Eugene and Meredith locked eyes as Ms. Beasley walked over.

"Sorry, boys, no eating on the bus," she said. "But don't worry— we'll be having lunch after the play." Then she went back to the front.

"Ha! I win!" Meredith cried. "Nobody breaks the rules while I'm around," she said. "Not even **EU-GERM.**"

Eugene sighed as he packed up his Boredom Destruction Kit. "Thank goodness I brought my nacho cheese," Charlie whispered. "Because this field trip is going to take a heroic dose of cheese and lots of patience."

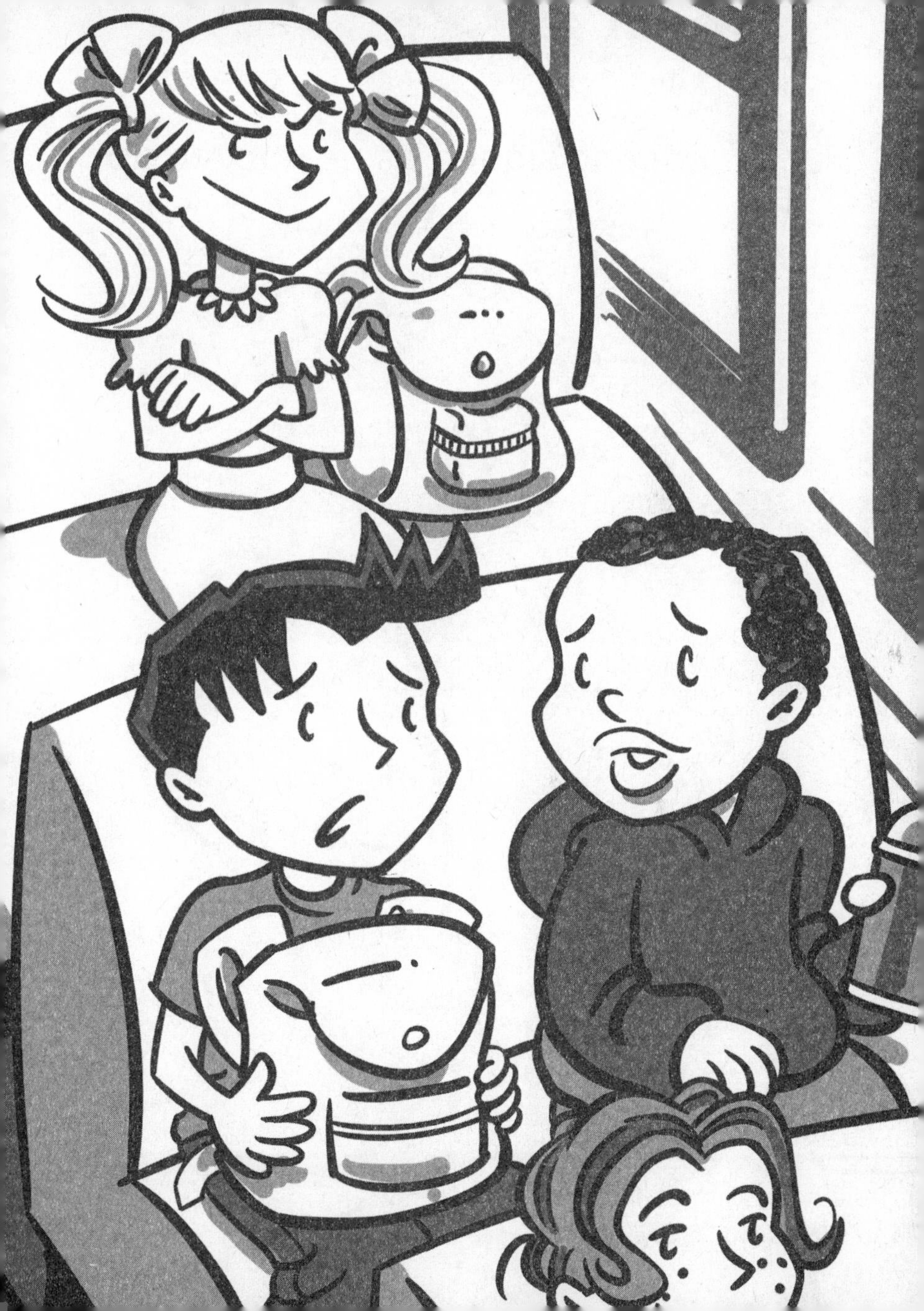

CHAPTER 3

Showtime!

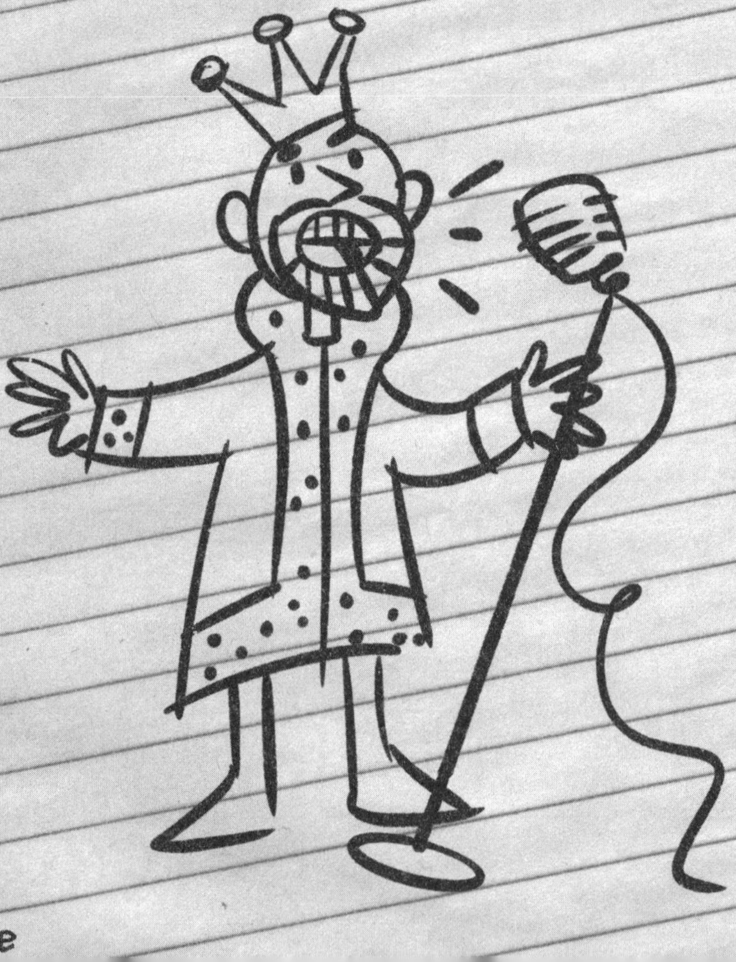

FINALLY!

Eugene looked up as they pulled up to the Sunnyview Playhouse.

"I thought we were going to Planet Boredom in a spaceship made of the Boredom Element!" he exclaimed.

The three-story building had a large dome for a roof and a golden lion on either side of the glass doors.

There was a banner over the entrance that said WELCOME, SUNNYVIEW ELEMENTARY SCHOOL! in bold red letters.

The kids quickly got off the bus and gathered under the sign.

"Okay, listen up, class," Ms. Beasley said. "This playhouse was built in 1858, making it one of the oldest buildings in town. Before we go in, here are the rules: no chitchatting, no fidgeting, and no bathroom breaks unless it's an emergency!"

WHAM! The list of noes hit Eugene like the pile of bricks that hit Super Dude in the face in Super Dude's Construction Special No. 2.

In the lobby, they were met by a man wearing a long coat and a Viking helmet with two big horns on it.

"Welcome to the Sunnyview Playhouse!" he bellowed in a deep voice. Then he stepped aside to let them into the theater.

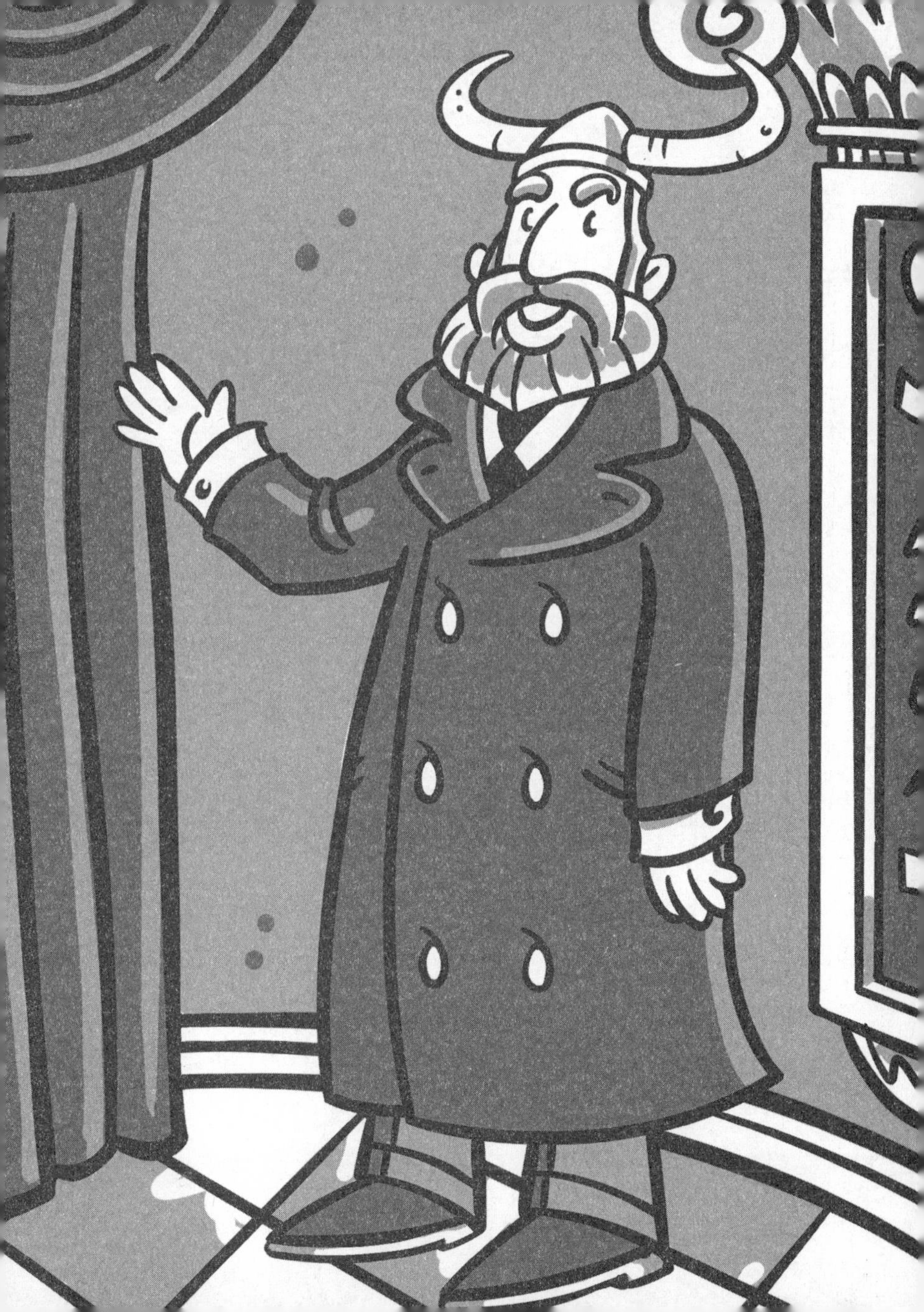

Eugene gasped when he entered the auditorium. "I hate to admit it, but . . . this *is* kind of cool!" he cried.

The dome-shaped room was

painted solid gold. It had a glass
chandelier that sparkled in the
light and red velvet curtains that
covered a big wooden stage.

"This is awesome!" exclaimed Charlie. "We have the best seats in the house!"

Hey! Maybe this play won't be so bad after all, Eugene thought.

As the trio sat down, the same man in the long coat came out onstage. This time he was wearing a puffy feather hat.

"Hear ye, hear ye! Today you shall hear a tale of happiness, doom, love, and romance!" he exclaimed.

EW.

Eugene squirmed in his seat. *Romance?* he thought.

BLEGH! NEVER MIND.

"Enjoy the show!" the man cried, and then he marched off.

As soon as the play began, Eugene's ears were filled with

old-timey words like "thee," "thine,"
and other weird *th* words. He was
so bored that when the speech
ended, Eugene stood up, ready to
leave.

"Hey, it's not over yet," Sally
said. "This is just the beginning."

HMPH. Eugene sighed and
sank back into his seat.

In the next scene, a knight bravely battled a bunch of bad guys, while a woman came out on a balcony and started singing about love and other mushy things. *SWOOSH! CLANK! CLANK!*

Okay. The battle scenes are kind of cool, but this is TOO much, Eugene thought.

Even with a sword fight going on, Eugene's eyes felt so heavy, he thought there were invisible weights on them.

I know this heavy feeling! Eugene thought. *Someone must be trying to bore me into the dreaded Bore Doom!*

He thought of Professor Yakkity-Yak, the villain who put people to sleep with his boring voice in Super Dude Campus Edition No. 14. If Eugene didn't do something soon, his brain was going to melt and leak out of his ears!

So he took a deep breath. It was time to use his Captain Awesome Breath of Awesomeness!

CHAPTER 4

Evil Wears Black!

By
Eugene

Eugene blew out a long, deep breath of air. If he could blow away all the words as they came out of the actors' mouths, the Bore Doom would be gone!

WHOOSHHH!

As if on cue, the actors stopped singing, and the curtains closed. It worked!

Yes! I saved the day! Eugene thought.

"We just finished the first act!" Ms. Beasley announced. "Wasn't that just wonderful?"

WHAT?
WE'RE ONLY HALFWAY?!

"Argh! That means there's a whole second act left!" Charlie said with a sigh.

"Not to worry! I shall defeat act two with another breath of my awesomeness!" Eugene declared.

But it turned out Ms. Beasley had other plans.

"We're going backstage to explore the magic of the theater!" she cried. Everyone followed her down the aisle and out through an exit by the side of the stage.

It was as busy as a beehive on the other side of the door. The kids watched as the stagehands moved scenery, light stands, electrical cords, and all kinds of fancy royal costumes.

"Oh my goodness! We're back-stage!" Sally whispered with glee.

But Eugene was not as amused.

"Class! I'd like to introduce you to the director," Ms. Beasley said as a man walked up. "This is Mr. Lucas Fudd."

A man with curly black hair, big black glasses, and a yellow sweater that looked a bit too tight waved hello.

"Here we go again," Eugene whispered to Charlie. "What makes this worse is that I'm starving!"

"Me too!" agreed Charlie.

"And me three," Sally replied.

"Thank you for coming today," Mr. Fudd said as he scanned the group.

Eugene's eyes widened. A yawn was building up in the back of his throat, and he couldn't stop it! *YAWNNNNN!*

As he quickly covered his mouth, Eugene saw something that sent shivers up his spine.

A man dressed in all black struggled with a large trunk. He carried it offstage as a string of loose jewels trailed behind him.

Eugene elbowed Charlie right away. "Hey! Did you see what I just saw?"

"What? Did I miss some snacks?" Charlie asked. "All I saw was a mysterious man dressed in black stealing a big trunk."

"You guys saw that too?" Sally asked, poking her head between the two boys.

"You bet we did!" Charlie cried in an excited whisper.

"I don't know about you guys, but my Awesome-Sense is telling

me that something evil is going on backstage . . . and it's dressed in black!"

The trio quickly huddled together so that no one else could hear.

"Now is the time to say it!" Charlie said, looking over at his best friend.

Eugene nodded.

Then, in his best superhero voice, he whispered, "Sunnyview Superhero Squad . . . assemble!"

CHAPTER 5

The Mystery Man in Black

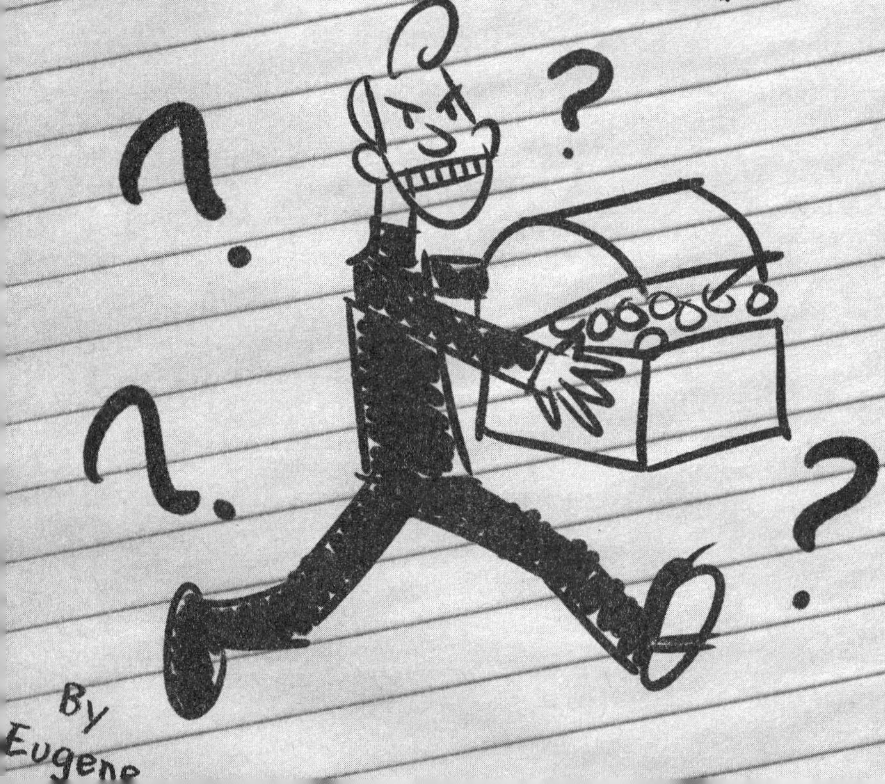

Mr. Fudd led the class off the stage and through a narrow door into the greenroom.

The trio waited until they were last in line; then, when everyone else went through the door, they bolted to the left.

"The Man in Black went this way!" Eugene cried, pointing to the floor. "That looks like a glove that fell out of the trunk!"

"I'm sure he's stealing it to take to his lair!" Charlie said as he opened his backpack. "We've got to hurry!"

UNZIP!
SPIN!
SUPERHERO!

Captain Awesome, Supersonic

Sal, and Nacho Cheese Man were now ready for action.

They ran down the narrow hallway, past some coiled rope and a box of giant light bulbs. At the end, the heroes needed to decide whether to turn left or right.

"The Man in Black went to the right!" Captain Awesome declared.

"Because according to Super Dude's Crime-Fighting Notebook, crooks always sneak out the back door."

"Of course!" Supersonic Sal said.

"Yes, let's do it!" Nacho Cheese Man cried. Then he pulled out a can

of cheese and squirted some in his mouth. "Cheese powers, activate!"

They turned the corner, but right away, the three heroes froze.

There were people everywhere, pushing racks of costumes in one direction and rolling tall lights in the other.

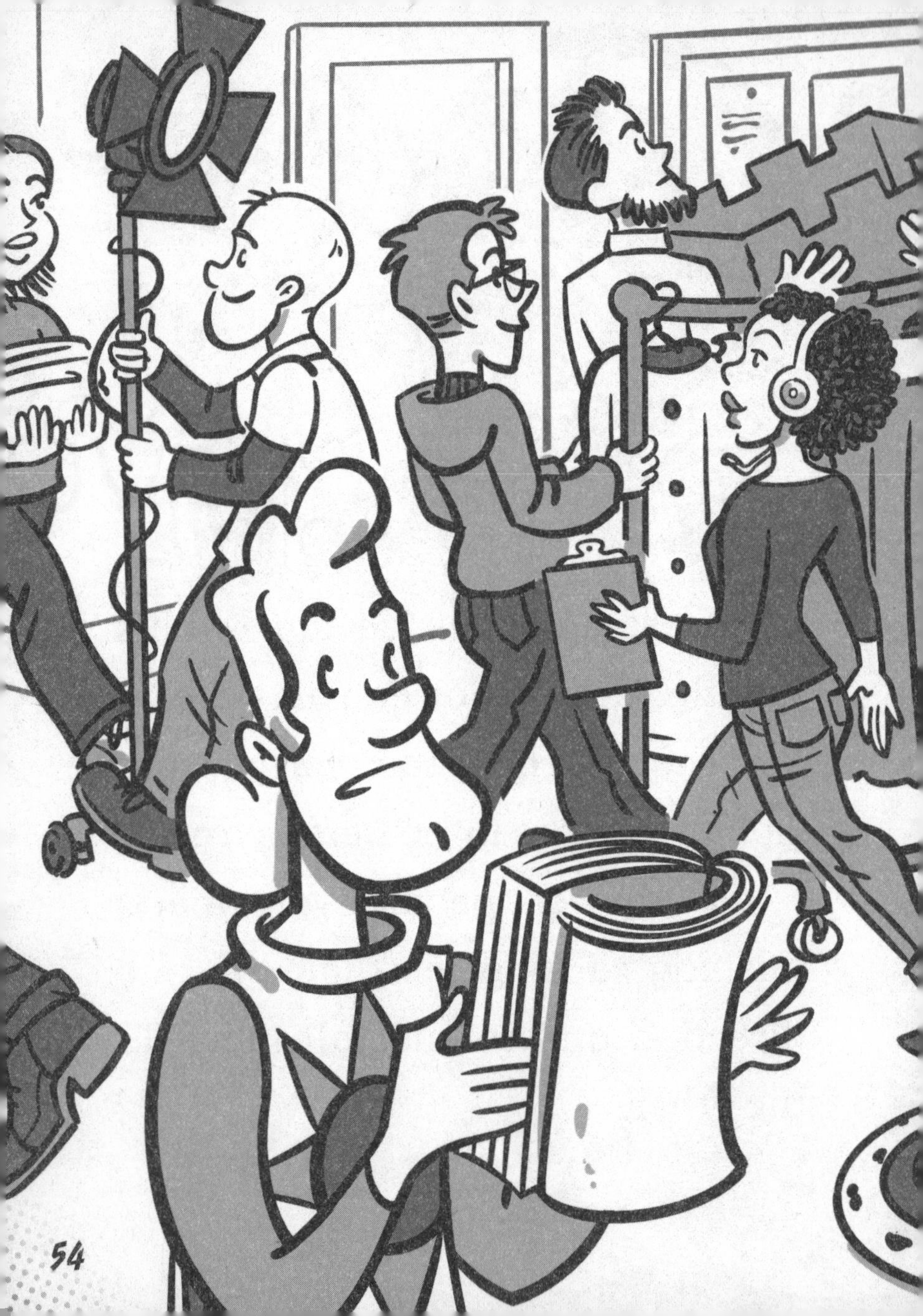

There was even a queen in a dark red robe sitting in front of a mirror, while a king fixed his beard.

"We've got to get through this chaos to stop the Man in Black!" Supersonic Sal said. "Or else the show can't go on!"

That's when Captain Awesome stood tall and called out loudly, "Hold fast, good citizens of the playhouse! Make way for the Sunnyview Superhero Squad!"

Everyone stopped what they were doing. Some workers even moved against the wall as the trio raced by.

"This way!" Captain Awesome cried.

"Good luck, superheroes!" the queen called out.

"You were great in the play, Your Majesty," Supersonic Sal said before running off. "The show WILL go on!"

By the time the heroes reached the end of a second hallway, the Man in Black had vanished!

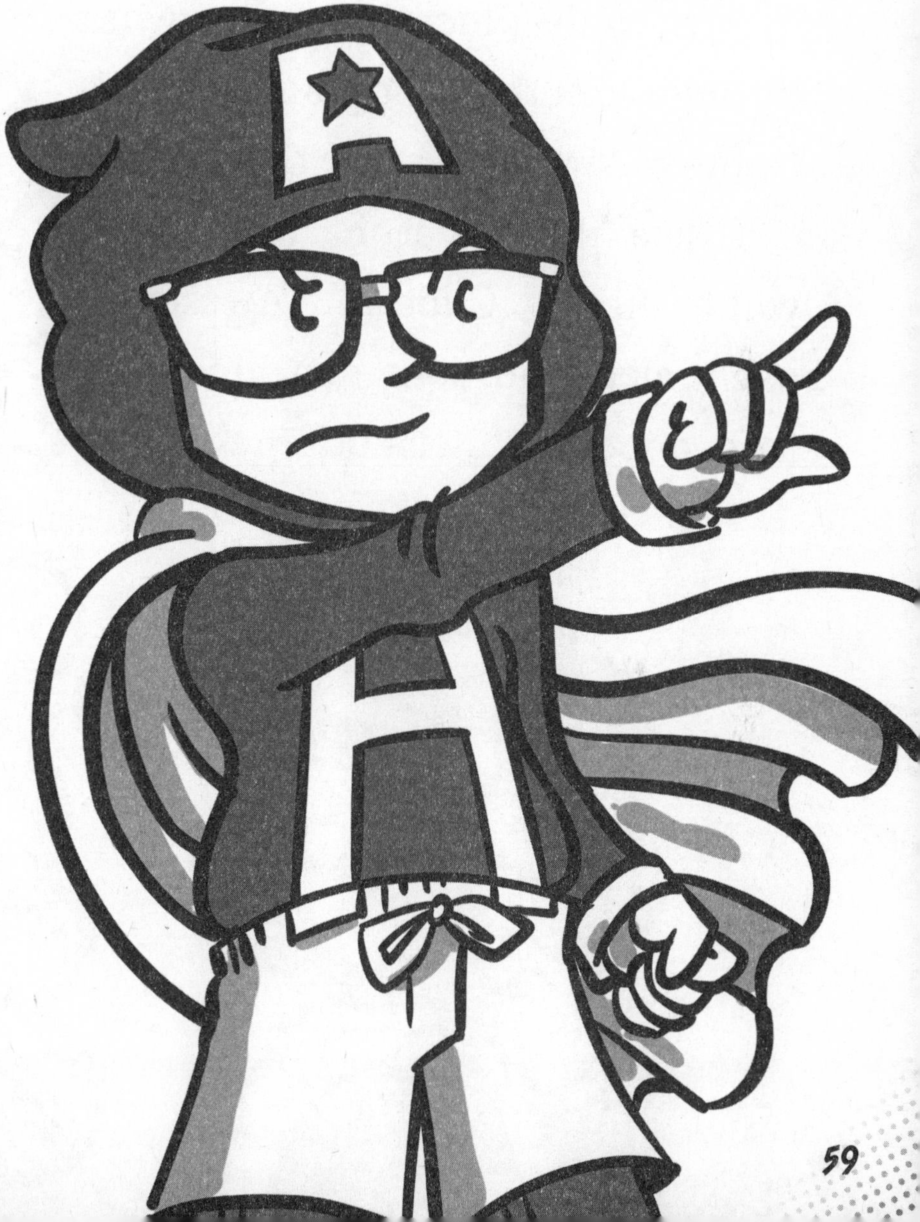

The only place left to go was through another big metal door. Captain Awesome knew this was it.

"The thief is right where we want him!" Captain Awesome exclaimed. "No door can hide evil from goodness! Let's go!"

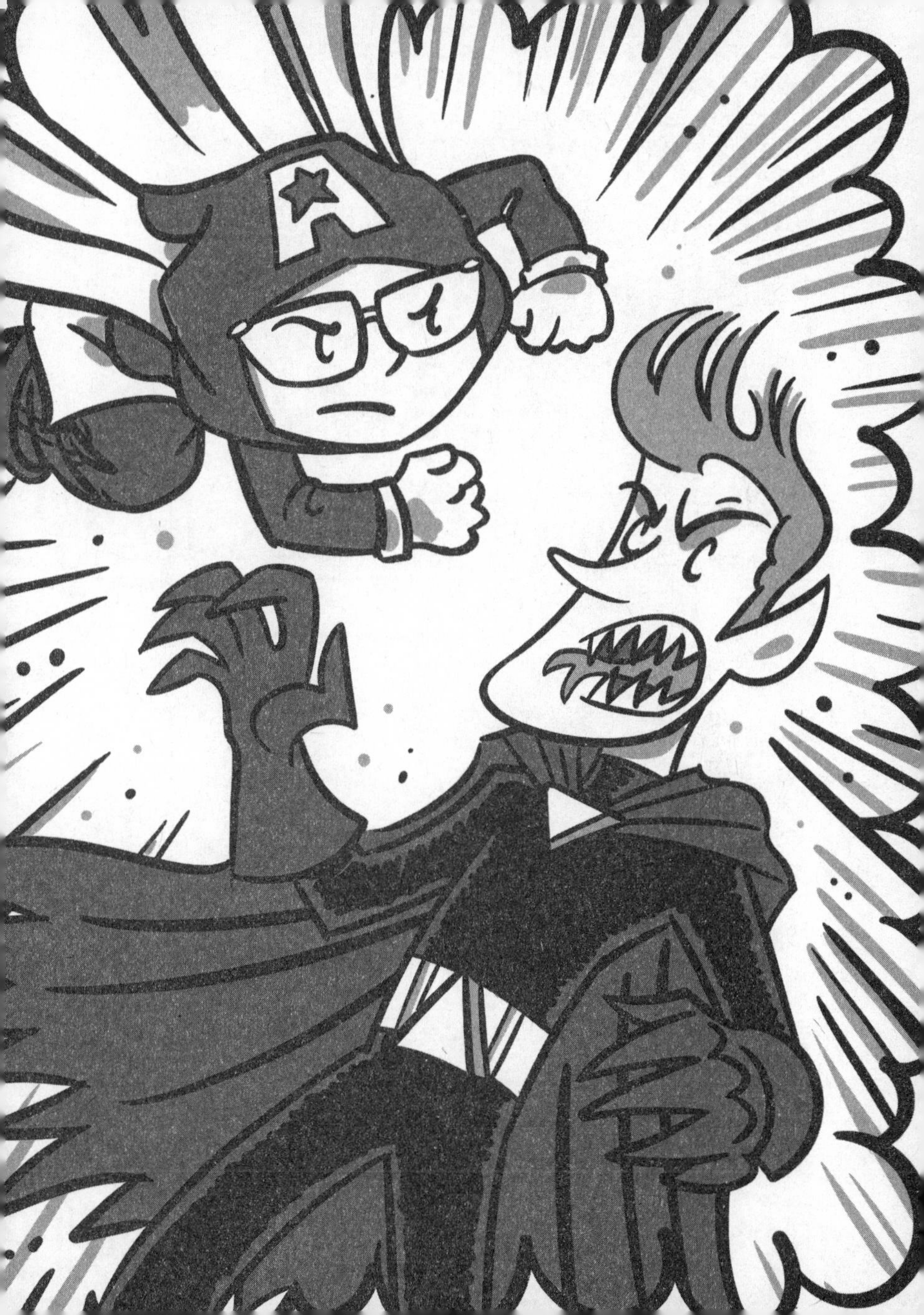

CHAPTER 6

Slimed by the Sinister Squid-tron!

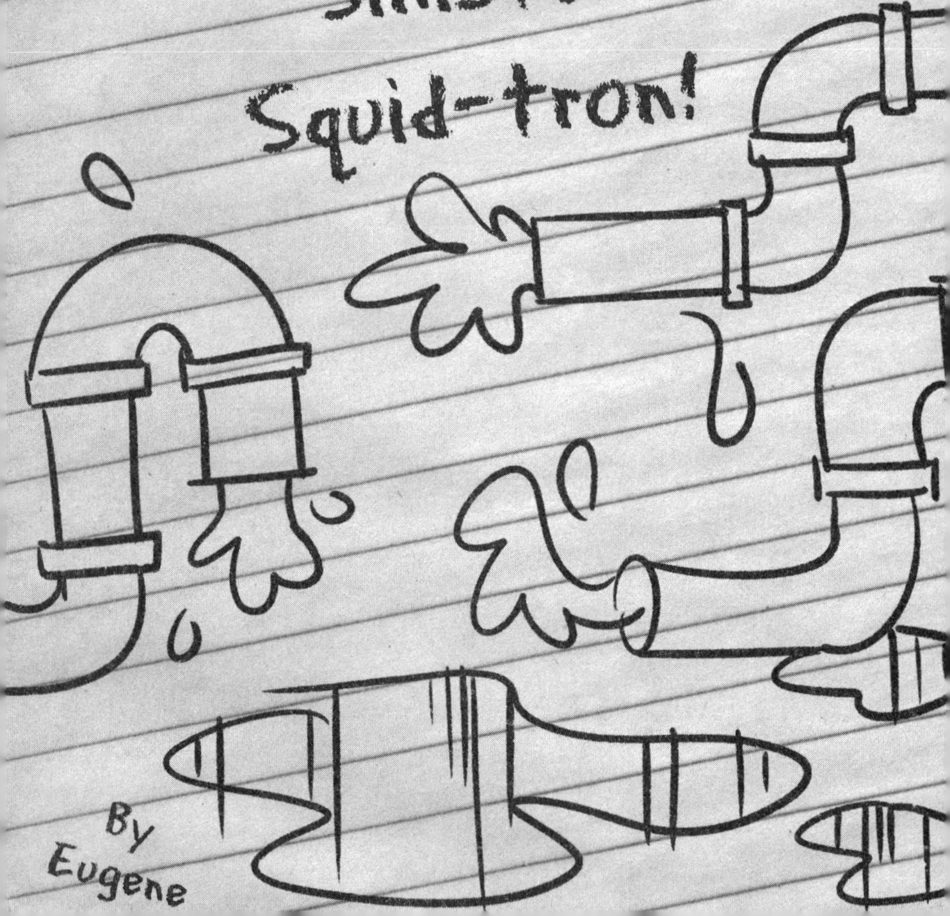

By Eugene

Captain Awesome opened the door, and the superheroes raced into a dark room. Right away, a loud noise echoed around them.

CLANK! CLANK! CLANK!

"Maybe we should stay on the *other* side of the door and let that clanking stay on *this* side of the door," Nacho Cheese Man said.

"No, we can't do that," Captain Awesome replied in a serious tone.

"It is the sworn duty of a superhero to look into all **_CLANKS_**, **_BANGS_**, **_BOOMS_**, and **_WOCKA-WOCK-WOO-BOING-ZOOMS!_**"

The trio nodded in agreement. They all knew that superheroes needed to be ready to battle even the weirdest noises.

So Nacho Cheese Man clenched his eyes shut as Captain Awesome slowly opened another door to reveal . . . another narrow hallway!

"Again?!" Captain Awesome gasped. "What kind of evil are we up against?!"

The trio quietly stepped into the dark hall. Long pipes lined the ceiling, and the walls were black. **CLANK! CLANK! CLANK!** The noise was back!

And this was proof: Whoever was hiding in the shadows knew how to be loud *and* super annoying.

That's when a light bulb went off in Captain Awesome's head. *Long pipes that look like arms . . . walls that are as black as ink . . . and constant clanking* and *clanging . . .*

"Guys! I think we've stumbled into the lair of the Sinister Squid-tron!"

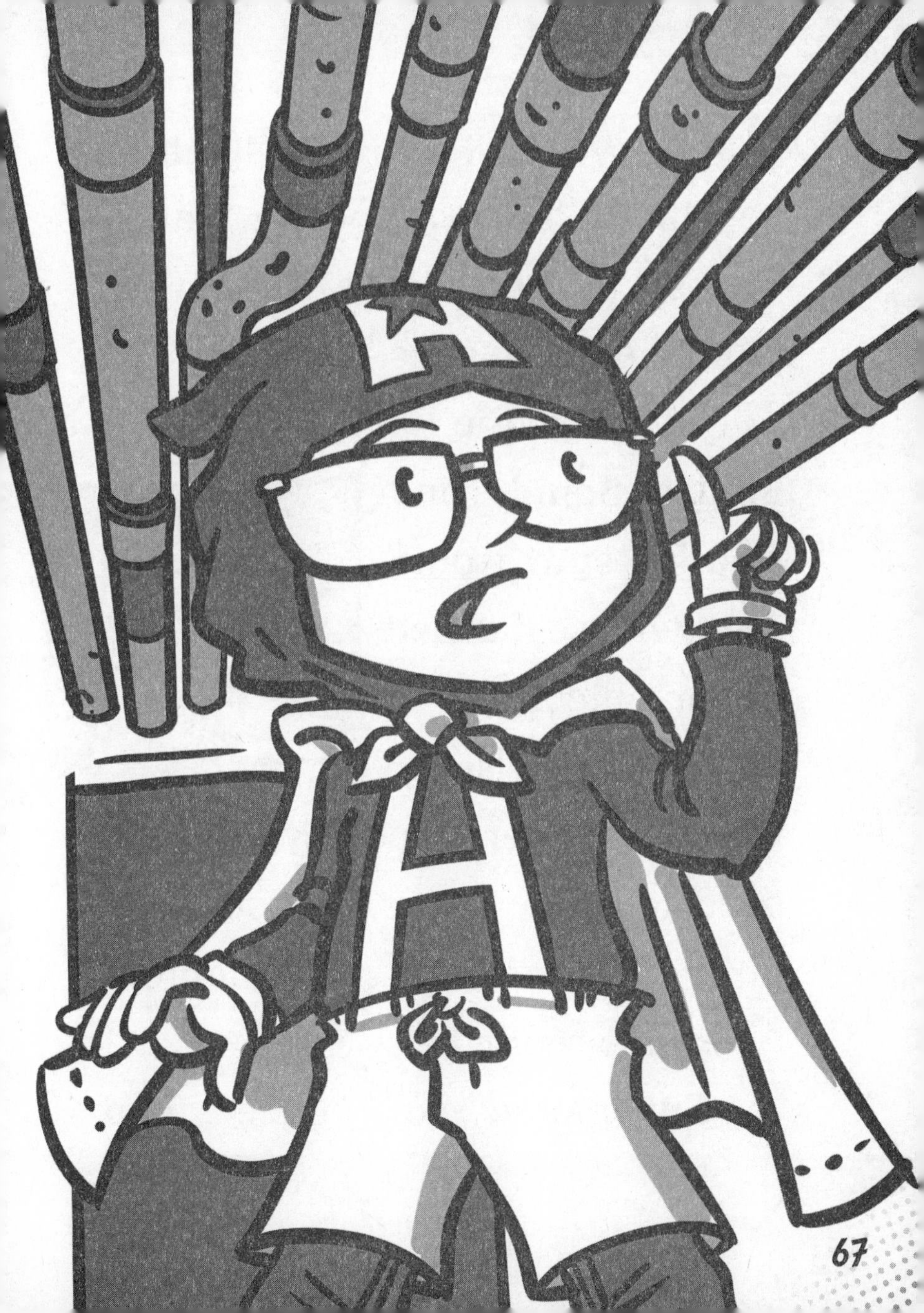

"Oh yeah? Then let's see how he likes Extra Kooler Ranch Cheese!" Nacho Cheese Man cried, pulling out two cans.

"Why is the Sinister Squid-tron stealing stuff from a playhouse?" asked Supersonic Sal.

"In the wise words of Super Dude: 'Evil doesn't need to make sense. It just needs an *e* followed by *-vil*,'" Captain Awesome replied.

Supersonic Sal nodded and

thanked Captain Awesome for the reminder. He was right. The forces of evil never made sense.

Then the heroes slowly walked forward, on edge for a sighting of Sinister Squid-tron's slimy Mega Tentacles.

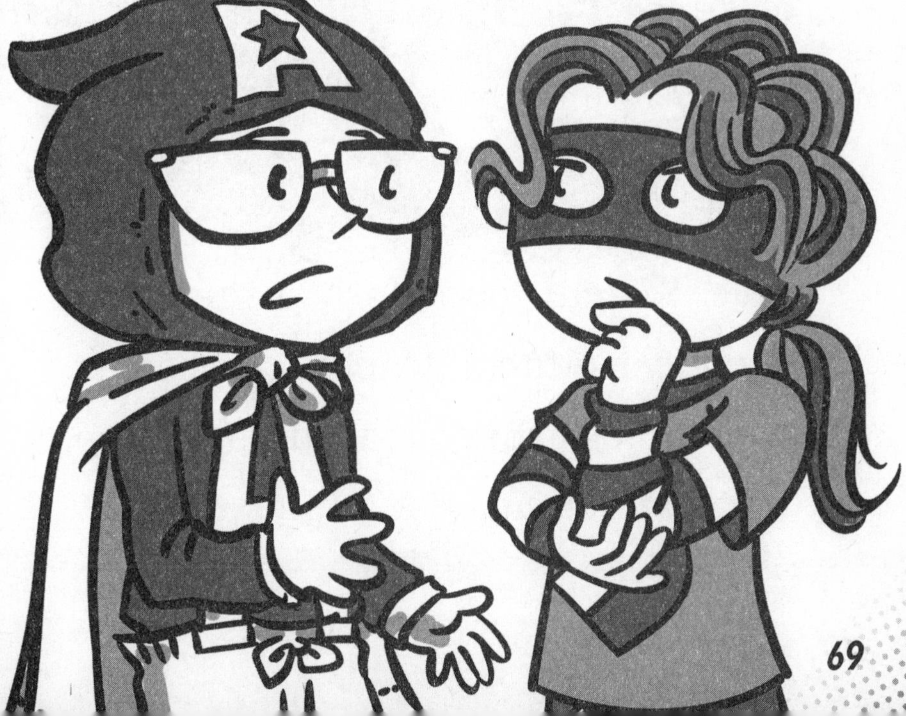

And that's when the noise came again.

CLANK! CLANK! CLANK!

"Watch out for a tentacle trouncer attack!" Captain Awesome yelled as they leaped into the shadows.

But this time the clanking wasn't the Sinister Squid-tron!

It was the . . .

VERY OLD WATER HEATER!

"Aw man, we were tricked! The Sinister Squid-tron will get to swim another day," Captain Awesome said with a sigh.

"But we still need to find the Man in Black!" said Supersonic Sal.

Captain Awesome pointed to the end of the hall. "He's probably behind that door!"

Nacho Cheese Man shook his head. "But what if it's another hallway? I really can't take such madness!"

"There's only one way to find out!" Supersonic Sal flung open the door, and the three heroes ran right into . . . their classmates!

Captain Awesome looked around as his friends helped him up. Somehow, they were back on their class tour with Mr. Fudd.

"Wait, if we're back where we started, that means that all those hallways are connected," Nacho Cheese Man whispered. "The Man in Black could be anywhere in the building now!"

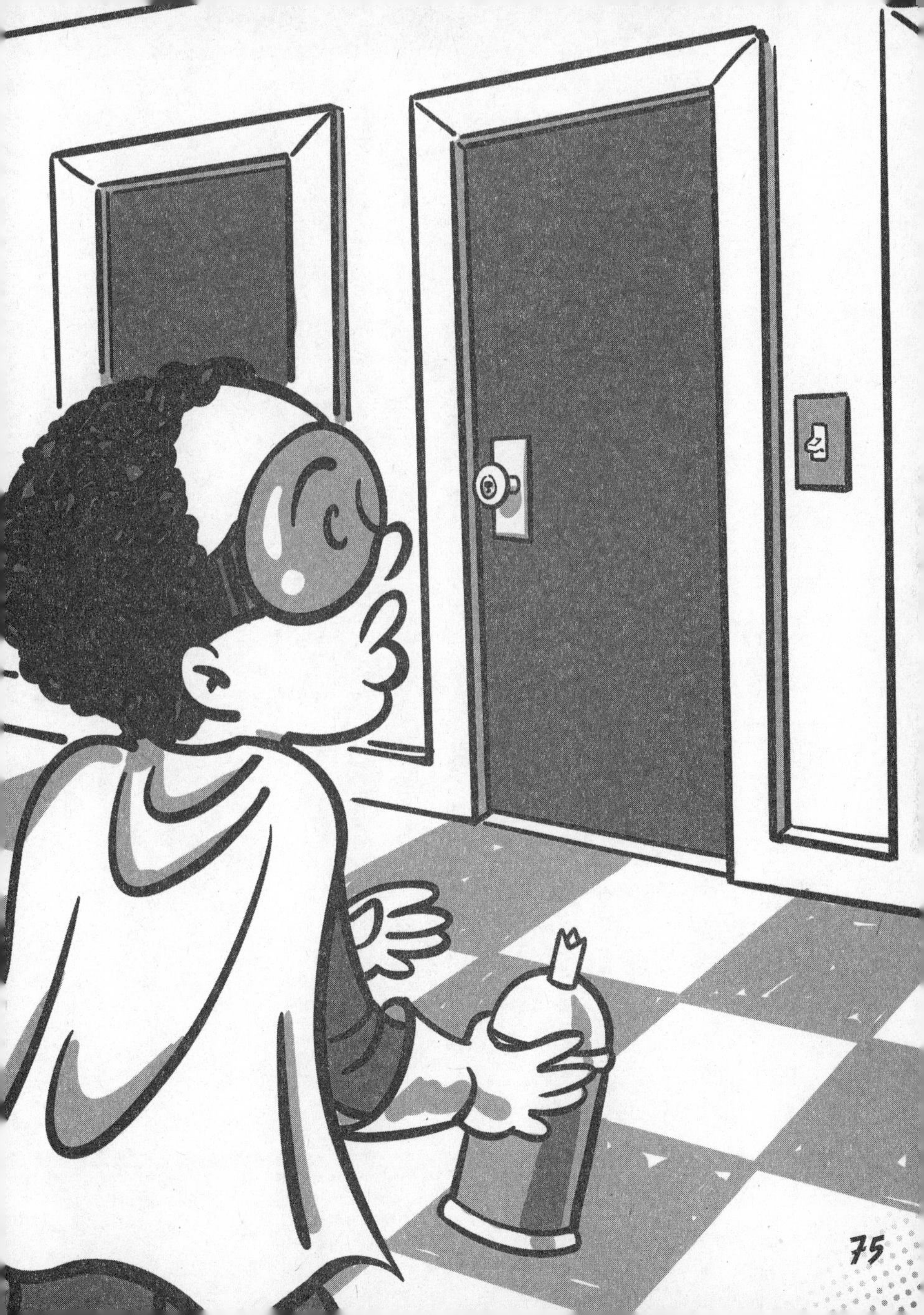

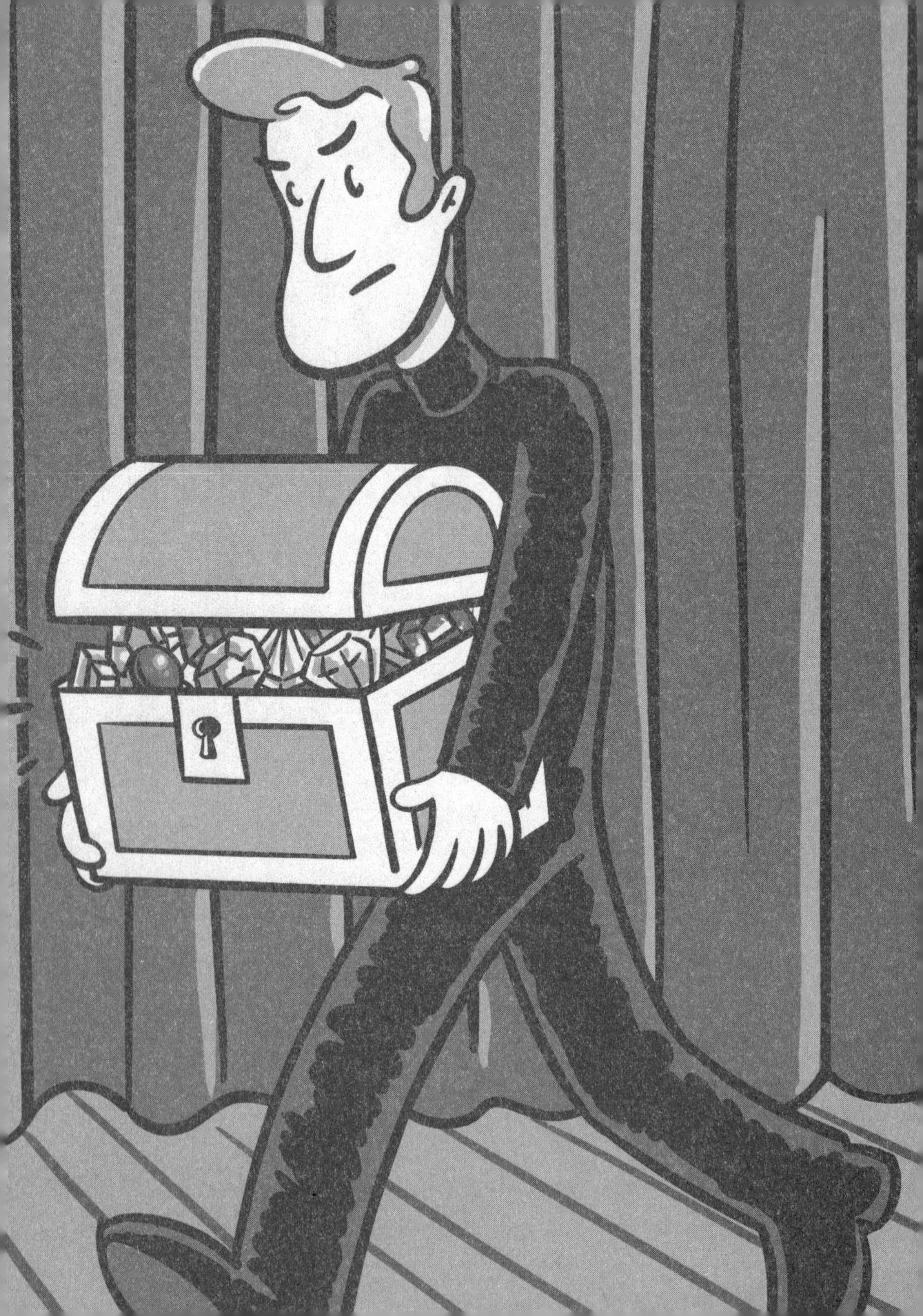

"Or . . . he could be right in front of us!" Nacho Cheese Man gasped as the Man in Black walked right onstage carrying the trunk full of stolen gems!

CHAPTER 7

Boredom by Any Other Name

HELLO
MY NAME IS
Boredom

By
Eugene

As they watched the thief come and go, Eugene, Sally, and Charlie quickly shoved their superhero costumes in their backpacks. They wanted to chase after the Man in Black, but Ms. Beasley insisted that it was time to sit back down.

"Wait. Who made up the rule that you could only save the planet during breaks?!" Sally huffed.

"SHHHHH!"

Meredith shushed them as she leaned forward in her chair. "It's bad enough I have to sit here behind you. Don't make me listen to your voices, too!"

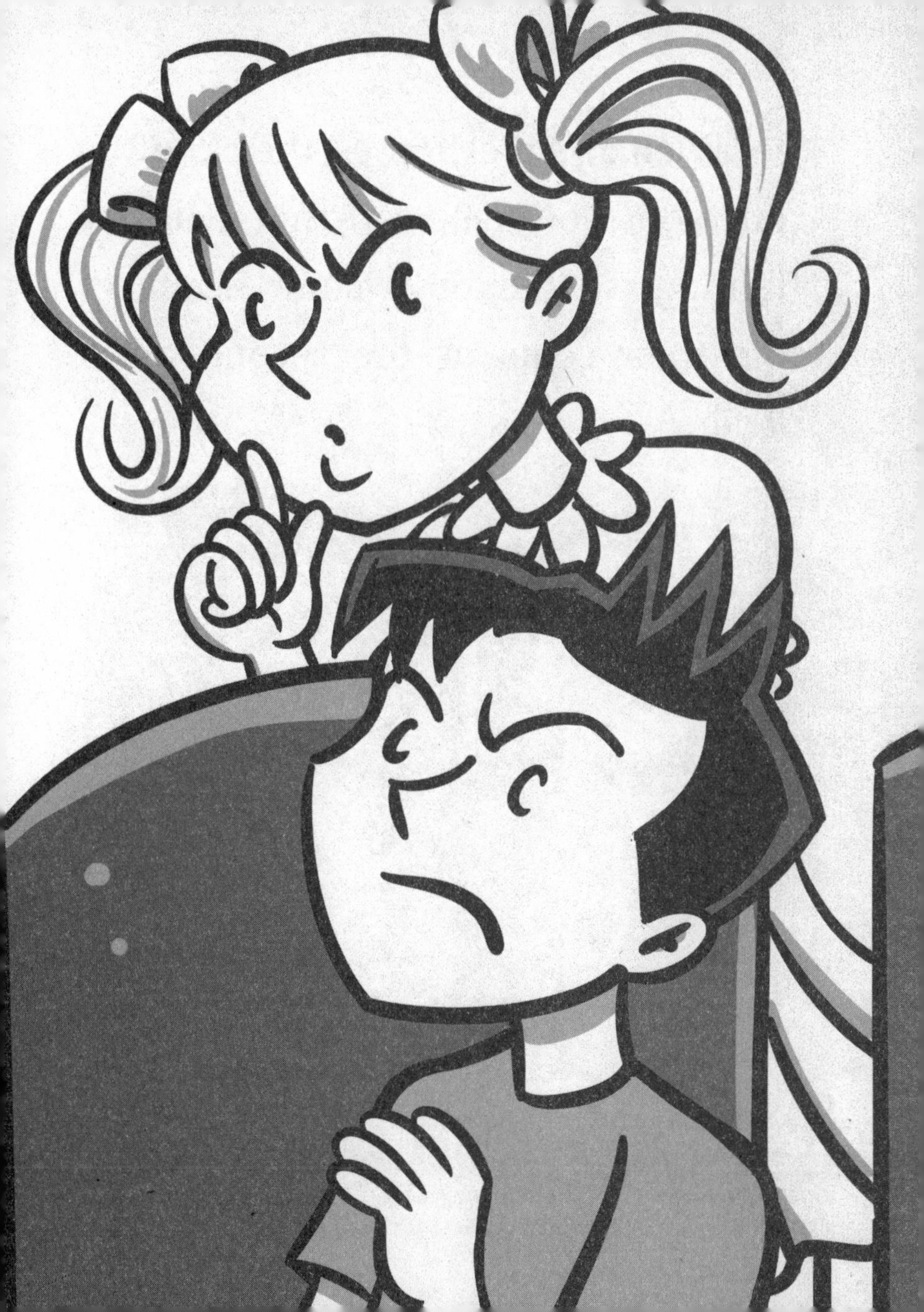

Even as superheroes, they knew that some battles were not worth fighting, so the boys sank deeper into their seats as the second act began.

Onstage, a man climbed a ladder to a woman's balcony. They were talking about roses and names, or maybe it was someone *named* Rose. Eugene wasn't exactly sure.

BUT THAT'S WHEN HE SAW THE MAN IN BLACK AGAIN!

"Hey! Did you see that?" Eugene gasped. He shook Charlie awake.

"What? Is the play over? Are we going home?" Charlie mumbled.

"Charlie, there's no time to go

home! Not when evil is eviling right before our eyes!" Eugene pointed to the Man in Black.

"What's the Man in Black doing on the stage . . . in the middle of the play?!" Charlie asked.

"Is he trying to steal the curtain?!" Sally chimed in.

"No, it's worse than that," Eugene replied. "He's going to rob the whole theater once the play makes everyone fall asleep!"

"Oh no! We can't just let him get away with it!" Sally cried. "How do we make sure Ms. Beasley doesn't see us?"

"We can do what Super Dude did in Super Dude number sixty-two!" Eugene piped up. "Remember how he created a super-soapy distraction?"

"But we don't have any super-soap," Sally said with a shrug.

"Yeah, but we have the next best thing!" Eugene replied. "Canned cheese and a nice clear aisle!"

Eugene looked over at Charlie and gave him a nod. So Charlie grabbed one can, placed it under the seat in front of him, and let go. **ZOOM!**

The can sped down the aisle all the way to the front row and hit the stage with a loud **BANG!**

"Let's go!" Eugene whispered.

With everyone in the theater distracted, the trio got on their hands and knees and quietly snuck out.

CHAPTER 8

The Pointer Finger of Justice!

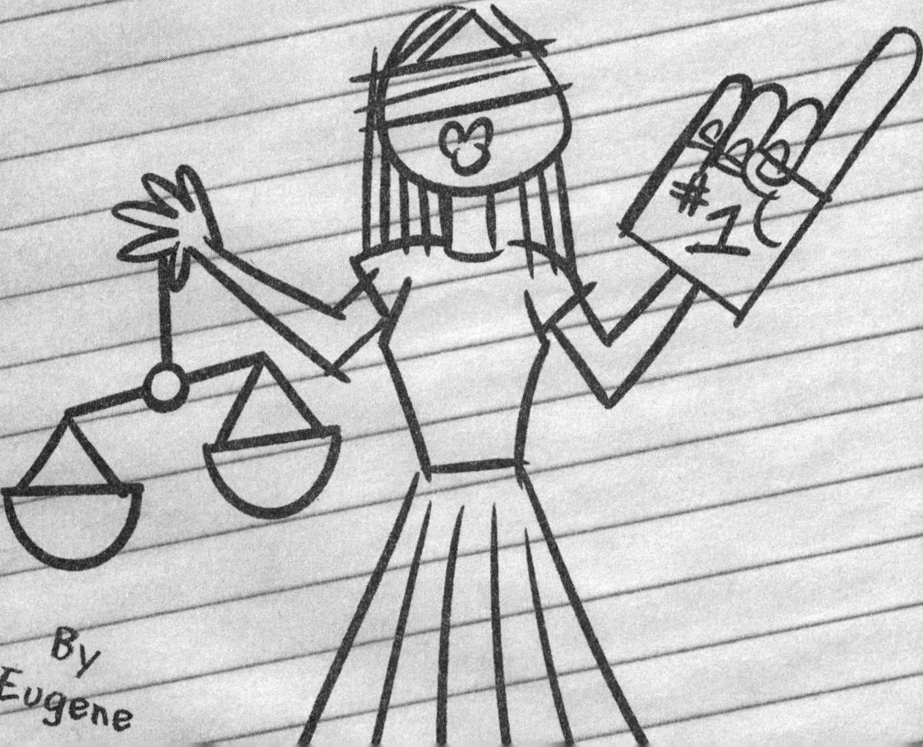

By Eugene

UNZIP!
SPIN!
SUPERHERO!

The heroic adventures of the Sunnyview Superhero Squad were back on!

"With all these hallways and doors, it's not going to be easy to find the Man in Black," Supersonic Sal said. "What's our plan, Captain Awesome?"

"We need to do the same thing Super Dude did in Super Dude number four hundred twenty-one. Even though Mac and Sneeze unleashed the Achoo-Choo Train of Doom, Super Dude stopped their plans by following the train tracks!"

"We have to look out for train tracks?" Nacho Cheese Man asked.

"Not train tracks . . . *villain* tracks! Look!" Captain Awesome pointed to a crown on the ground. "The Man in Black must've dropped it when he was making his escape!"

So they grabbed the crown and then charged down the hall. When they got to the next room, their mouths dropped to the floor.

There were swords, diamond tiaras, gold goblets, shields, and so much more!

"Look! The trunk that the Man in Black took is here!" Supersonic Sal cried.

"This room must be a secret teleportation zone that's connected to the Man in Black's secret lair!" Captain Awesome cried. "Quick! Find the controls and turn them off!"

But before the heroes could make another move, someone

raced through the door! It was . . .
THE MAN IN BLACK!

He placed several necklaces
and some gold coins on a shelf.

"Ah! I've been looking for this!"
he said as he picked up the crown.

That's when the trio jumped
out of the dark.

"Halt in the
name of good-
ness!" Captain
Awesome called out, stabbing his
Pointer Finger of Justice at the Man
in Black. "We found that crown! It
belongs to the playhouse!"

Captain Awesome's heroic words made the Man in Black jump.

"Wow! How did you find this?" the Man in Black said, surprised. "I've been looking all over for this. Thank you!"

And with that, he raced away as quickly as he had arrived.

"Wait . . . did he just thank us for stopping him? Did we just win against the Man in Black?" Nacho Cheese Man asked.

"We sure did! And he left everything untouched, too," Sally replied.

"This proves that no bad guy can stand up to my Pointer Finger of Justice!" Captain Awesome said as he held up his finger.

CHAPTER 9

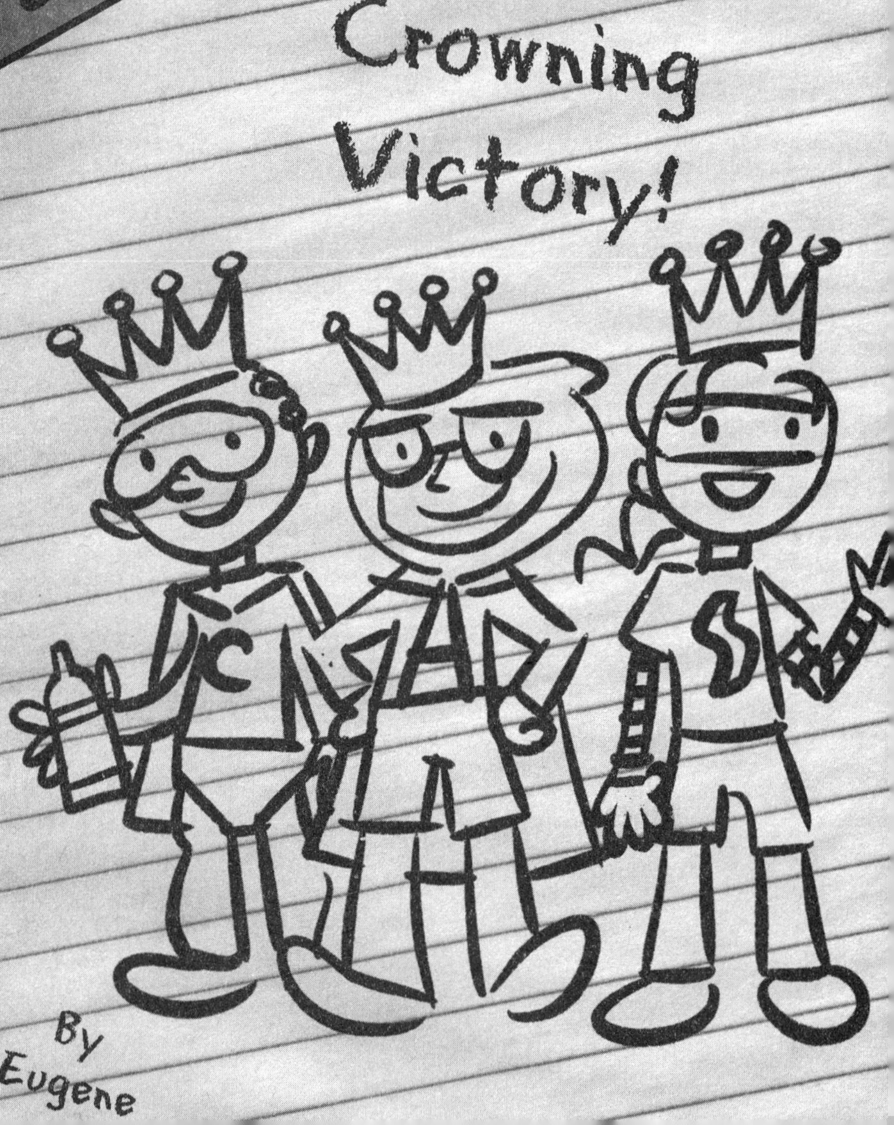
Crowning Victory!
By Eugene

After a quick change back into their school clothes, Eugene, Sally, and Charlie snuck to their seats. They had defeated the Man in Black before the play was even over!

They returned just in time to watch the last epic sword fight. After that, the curtain closed, and everyone in the audience burst into applause.

Even though he had missed a good chunk of the mushy parts, Eugene had to admit that the last fighting scene was totally cool. He and his friends got up and clapped as loudly as they could.

"Bravo! Encore!" Meredith shouted behind them.

When the clapping died down, Mr. Fudd took the stage.

"Thank you, everyone!" he said. "Please, let's give it up for our wonderful actors!"

The cast came back onto the stage and took a bow. They were met by another round of applause. Eugene noticed that the man who played the prince was wearing the crown they'd saved from the Man in Black!

"There are so many more people working hard to make each play we perform the best it can be," Mr. Fudd continued. "I'd like to introduce you to all the behind-the-scenes members of our team who make all of this possible."

One by one, the crew members came out to center stage and explained each of their jobs.

The head costume designer talked about making the costumes. Then came the hair-stylist and the musical director, who handled everyone's hair and all the music. After that, a set designer explained how they built the sets, while the lighting

designer showed how she used light to change the mood on the stage.

"Wow. I never knew there was so much involved in making a play," Eugene whispered to his friends.

"And now, last but not least, the final member of our crew," Mr. Fudd said, and motioned to the side of the stage.

GASP!
SHOCK!
GASP AGAIN!

Eugene jumped to his feet and shouted, "Look! It's the Man in Black!"

"That's right! It's our very own
man in black—Steve the prop
master!" Mr. Fudd announced.

"Prop Master?! That's a more evilly sounding name than the Man in Black!" Charlie whispered to Eugene.

"Can any of you guess what job the prop master has?" Mr. Fudd asked.

"Does he steal everything in the playhouse and teleport it to his evil base?" Eugene answered.

"Um, no. Why don't you handle this one, Steve?" Mr. Fudd said.

"Sure thing! As lead prop master, I get all the items we need, like swords, books, gems, and even a *crown*. Of course, most props are not real at all," Steve explained.

"And if I can't buy a prop we need, I get to make it myself."

"So . . . you're not a bad guy in black?" Eugene asked, confused.

"Nope!" Steve chuckled. "I dress in black so I don't distract anyone if I have to set up some props while the play is going on. You may have seen me in the background during the play. I had to place a dagger on one of the tables."

"Wow. What an awesome job!"
Charlie said.

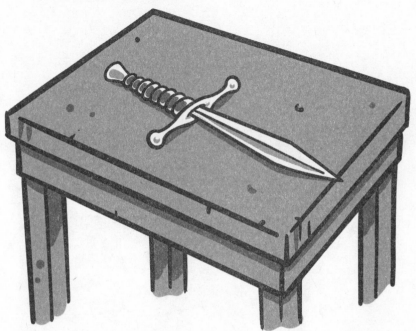

"Yeah, but guess what? Props go missing in the middle of a show sometimes. We were in trouble today until three heroes saved the day just in time!" Steve said. Eugene and his friends couldn't help but smile.

The Sunnyview Superhero Squad may not have stopped an evil villain from robbing the playhouse this time, but they did make sure that the show could go on without a hitch for their entire class, and in many ways, that was even more *MI-TEE!*

CHAPTER 10

The Peas of Evil!

By
Eugene

Eugene sat at the dinner table and stared at his plate of food. Even though he had defeated the likes of **QUEEN STINKYPANTS**, **MR. DROOLS**, and **THE SHUSHER**, at home he was helpless before the evil peas on his plate.

"You'll never beat me, little green villains!" Eugene whispered as he mushed the peas with his fork.

"So how was the field trip?" his mom asked, interrupting his battle with the evil peas. "Did you enjoy the play?"

Eugene stopped mashing the peas and looked up.

"Well, it wasn't the field trip I wanted to go on. And it wasn't even a place I wanted to go to. And it wasn't a thing I wanted to see. Or do. *Ever.* I really thought it was going to be the field trip of doom . . . but there were some pretty cool parts."

His parents nodded as Eugene continued.

"There were epic battles and

guys with swords and some guys who didn't have swords . . . but I bet they all *wanted* swords."

"Sounds impressive." His mom smiled. "Why were they fighting?"

"Oh, I think because of some epic doom, along with love and other mushy things," Eugene explained.

Eugene thought about telling his parents about the Man in Black and how Captain Awesome, Supersonic Sal, and Nacho Cheese

Man tried to stop him from robbing the playhouse—only to discover that he actually worked there.

But then Eugene realized that would be giving away too much. He and Captain Awesome appearing at the same play was too much of a

coincidence, and the last thing he wanted was for his parents to suspect something weird.

Plus, Eugene remembered what Super Dude would say in a moment like this: "Never do anything that will give your secret identity away, because then your superhero-ness won't be a secret . . . and there's not much fun in that."

Eugene smiled as he defeated the last of the evil green peas.